the Huffler

the Huffler

Jill Paton Walsh

illustrations by Juliette Palmer

Farrar, Straus and Giroux

New York

Library of Congress Cataloging in Publication Data
Paton Walsh, Jill.   The huffler.
[1.   Canals—Great Britain—Fiction   2.   England—
Fiction]   I.   Palmer, Juliette.   II.   Title.
PZ7.P2735Hu3   [Fic]   75–25917
ISBN 0–374–33505–2

For the navigators of the

Mary Beatrice

the Huffler

I would never have had the courage for it myself. It was my cousin Harry who did it. She was eleven when she did it, and I was eleven when she told me about it; though by that time she was nearly grown-up herself. I was having a really dreadful time that summer, staying with cousin Harriet, and so dreadfully, awfully bored I thought I could hear my hair growing.

It wasn't exactly Harry's fault. The trouble was Edward. Edward was some family friend of Aunt Edith's—or, rather, the son of some friend of hers, and he was, we were told, madly suitable as someone for Harry to fall in love with and marry, and he liked her very much, so he had come to stay in Aunt Edith's big house in Warwickshire to see a lot of Harry, and try to win her affections. But Aunt Edith was ill—not what I'd call ill, with a fever and a furry tongue, and unable to eat even chocolate cake, but the sort of ill that meant she had to lie on a sofa under the open windows, sighing and reading

every other page of a book; and so although she could "keep an eye on the young people," as she put it, when they were sitting on the other sofa, heads down over some puzzle or game, and giggling together, she couldn't walk out with them. And, it seems, the more people would like to be alone together when they are trying to win each other's affections, the less they may be, so someone is needed to follow them around, just getting frightfully in the way—and, yes, you've guessed it: the someone was me. Aunt Edith had borrowed me specially to go walking with Harry and Edward, and pointed out to my mother how good the country air would be for me. And she did give us scrumptious teas, and smile a lot, and say "Thank you, Kate" when she asked me to do things, but I don't think anyone had troubled to consider how *very* uncomfortable it is to be sent running off all the time after people who would much rather you were not there.

We were all three walking on the canal bank, when Harry first mentioned it, on our way to find a good place for a picnic. It was Harry who had suggested the canal. Edward had looked dubious, and mentioned Shooters Wood, but now we were here he said, "I say, Harriet, what a topping place!" I thought it was rather good too, especially the little bridge, made of rosy-red brick, with a parapet of stone, and a cast-iron plate saying "47" on it, at which we had left the lane and climbed down onto the towpath. The bridge tapered a little toward the water, so that its reflection made a figure of eight when you looked back at it from the towpath.

It was a very prickly, uncomfortable sort of afternoon, in spite of us both liking Harry's canal so much, and, just for once, it was not because Edward and Harry were talking together all the time and taking no notice of me. And it was not because the only notice they were taking of me was to try and find ways to get rid of me, like "Go and see if there are mushrooms in that field, Kate," or "Oh, Kate, I've forgotten my shawl, just run back to the house and get it for me, will you?" No, Harry was paying me plenty of attention that day, pointing out flowers and butterflies beside the path, and it was "Look, Kate!" instead of "Look, Edward!" for the dragonfly, and the heron, though he did get the kingfisher pointed out to him. But somehow they were a bit cross with each other, though not in the least admitting it, and the prickly feeling made me feel uncomfortable too.

When we came to the next little bridge, we crossed by it into the hayfield on the opposite bank from the towpath, for Harry said we mustn't sit on the towpath, or we'd be frightfully in the way. While we lingered on the bridge, dawdling in the heat, and looking into the green water, some boats came by. First we saw a horse on the towpath, plodding toward us. It had its nose in a brightly painted can of oats, and a tiny girl in a scruffy overall trotted beside it, leading it, and holding on by a string of colored wooden beads which the horse wore, Harry said, to stop the harness rubbing. Behind the horse stretched the towrope, and at the end of the towrope the black prow of a narrow-boat came nosing around the corner, and behind that a second one.

"The butty boat!" said Harry. "And beautifully van-dyked."

"*Van-dyked!* It's painted like a tea-tray!" said Edward, laughing.

"Nevertheless," said Harry, "that's what they call it."

The boats were laden deep into the water, so that the names on their front ends were almost

washed by the gentle ripple they plowed on the glassy surface. At the front of each boat was a painted board, decorated with bunches of roses, and a castle standing by a winding waterway; down the center of the boats were rows of stout posts, painted like harlequins with gaudy triangles, and along the posts a line of planks was laid, and green side cloths were held almost over the cargo by ropes laced over and over these boards. At the back of the leading boat was a tiny cabin, with a cluster of children sitting on the roof, and a bronzed dark-haired workingman leaning on a huge upswept red and yellow tiller stood at the cabin door, thrusting the tiller sideways to bring his boat around the bend. The tiny child leading the horse squinted up at us, against the sunlight, and said, "Mornin'" from underneath the brown handkerchief she wore on her head. We watched them cast off the rope and glide smoothly under the bridge before hitching up the horse again the other side. When the first boat was through, it pulled its butty boat through behind it, and the butty boat was being steered by a tough-looking girl in a white cotton apron, very brown and dirty, with bare head and bare feet, who looked sharply away from meeting our eyes, and did not answer when Edward bid her "Good morning."

"I ran away on one of those once," said Harry.

"Oh, tell me another, Harriet!" said Edward, grinning.

"True, quite true," said Harry. "Mother said I wasn't to tell you about it on any account, for it makes me seem such a vagabond; but I think I *shall* tell you, all the same, for you might as well know what I'm really like."

"I do know what you're like," said Edward, vastly amused. "You're not the sort to run off with a barge-man!"

"It wasn't a number one I ran off with," said Harry, plucking a stem of grass and smiling slightly. "It was his butty boy. Come on, let's take the basket and rug into the shade of that big tree, and I'll tell you about it."

So we spread out the cloth in the mown hay in the shade, and set out on it all the good things that Aunt Edith's cook had prepared for us, and while we ate, Harry told us about the dreadful thing she had once done.

·

Harry said the trouble with her was, she got bored too easily. (How like me, *I* thought!) She hated being a girl, expected to mind very much what she put on each morning, even though there was never anywhere to go. She had a very strict, dull governess to teach her all her lessons, so she didn't even go out to go to school. And then, when she was eleven, her father announced that the family was going to move. He didn't say where, or when, just that they

were going quite soon and he hoped that Harry
would be particularly good, because her mother and
all the servants would have quite enough to do without having to trouble themselves about her. Being
good, Harry said, meant keeping right out of the
way, and asking no questions. Even Susan, her
nurserymaid, who was always gentle and kind with
her, was too busy to talk, and the governess took no
interest in her, but simply set Harry page after page
of sums to do all by herself, while she wrapped up
each piece of china in the whole house in newspaper,
and packed things one by one into tea chests.

Harry just sat over her sums, and daydreamed.
She thought of the thrill of living in a new place, of
all the new things and faces that moving would
bring. And most of all she dreamed of a house with a
view from the windows, from the schoolroom window especially, and from her own bedroom, so that
even when she wasn't allowed out, which was often,
she could look out at least. And the view she
dreamed of was of the sea, the wide blue sea. It
wasn't entirely moonshine either, Harry told us rue-
fully; she had heard someone mention "near Shipton" as where they were going, and she thought
Shipton would be a seaport. So Harry pictured the
sea for herself. She had never seen it. But in her
father's study there was a big oil painting which
showed the sea, covered all over with curly waves,
and swarming with ships of all sorts and sizes, and

bordered by wharves and quays with armies of swarthy men rolling barrels and heaving bales, so of course Harry thought the sea would be a splendid thing to have in view from a window—as good as a magic lantern show.

And then when they got to the new house, it was not by the sea at all, but in deep country.

It was a tall rose-red brick mansion, closed in on one side by a thick wood of tall trees, and with a dark dense hedge of holly screening it from the road. And it had a garden, a stretch of green lawn, but even that was not open, but closed in by a steep green grassy bank running just beyond the fence at the bottom of the garden, and entirely blocking out from view any prospect of fields or lanes or coppices beyond. Worst of all, Susan, although she had packed her things like all the other servants, and set out from the old house a day early, did not appear in the new house. The governess said that Harry was far too old to need a nurserymaid now, and Susan had gone to another family with young babies who needed caring for. Harry cried for three days, and told everyone, even her father, when he asked her how she liked her new home, that it was horrible, like a prison, and that made everyone cross with her, for they were all bustling around to make it nice, and her mother liked it a lot; it was just Aunt Edith's sort of thing—secluded, and peaceful and somewhat grand.

Harry spent most of her three days of weeping alone, locked in her bare new schoolroom, which had not even linoleum on the floor as yet, or anything unpacked to sit on, but only a pile of boxes in the middle of the floor. On the third day Harry had stopped moping and crying, and so she was let downstairs to see the beautiful new drawing room, where the grownups were to have such serene good times together, and to take tea with her mother. Aunt Edith said if Harry was good and quiet, she could come down for drawing-room tea every day from now on; but the picture of the sea had been hung over the mantel shelf of the drawing-room fire, and Harry no sooner clapped her eyes on it than she cried again, and so she was banished once more, and had to have her tea in the kitchen with Cook, who told her that it was very natural to be upset by all the goings on, and she, Cook, was upset too, and couldn't lay her hands on any pot, pan, or ladle when she wanted it, but that Harry and she would both find their way about, by and by.

Harry's father thought she looked pale and wan with all that crying upstairs, and so she was ordered out the next day, to play in the garden till lunch time, whether she liked it or not. Harry didn't like it much. The garden seemed sunk in green walls of tree or grass, and almost full, at that early hour, of blocks of deep shadow. Harry looked resentfully at the tall green bank beyond the fence, and then she sat down on the wet grass, and, closing her eyes, she imagined the landscape beyond—full of roads and fields, and farms and a wide, wide river going down to the shore, and right at the back a blue ocean, crowded with ships—steamers sporting their fluffy white smoke plumes, and lovely sailing ships. And when she opened her eyes again to scowl at the horrid green bank, there along the top of it a boat was moving by.

It was moving slowly and silently. Harry couldn't see the horse, or the towrope on the path the far side of the boat from where she sat; and it was a boat such as she had never seen before, or even imagined: like the ones we had just seen, long and black, and with beautiful painted posts in bright colors rising amidships. And when the back of the boat at last came into view from behind a willow tree, it had a little painted cabin, with a brass-bound black chimney, and a painted jug standing on the roof, and "THOMAS JEBB CARRIER BRAUNSTON" written on the side in handsome painted letters, with a brass-bound porthole in the middle. Harry could see a painted tiller, with a horsetail plume flying bravely behind it, and, most astonishing of all, she could see, leaning on the tiller, a little boy in a tattered shirt and colored suspenders, not much—no, *definitely* no older than Harry herself.

Harry was thunderstruck. How could a boat sail through the green grass, and the stems of meadow-

sweet? How? How possibly? She leaped up, and just
before the boat disappeared from view, she reached
the garden fence, and scrambled over it—it was made
of posts and rails like a farm gate, and very easy to
climb—and raced up the embankment, slipping and
sliding on the wet grass, and clinging with hands as
well as feet, and gained the top. The bank was brim-
ful of brown water, and edged with flowers and
reeds. It carried the canal across a little fold in the

land. On the far side from Harry's garden was a towpath, and along the towpath a horse was plodding,
wearing, it seemed to Harry's baffled gaze, for the
horse was now some way distant, a white lace cap
like a grandmother, and it was pulling not one boat
but two, of which pair Harry had seen the second
one going by, and the second one did indeed have
at the tiller a small boy, with his face and arms
burned brown by wind and sun.

"Hey!" cried Harry, staggering to her feet, breathless at the top of her climb. "Hey, stop!"

"Stop?" said the boy, turning very bright blue eyes on her, and pushing his cap back from a mass of dark curls, to scratch his head in bafflement. "Can't stop, even I'd reason to; and you ain't no reason."

"But I want to talk to you!" yelled Harry, stamping her foot. "I want to ask you . . ." The boat was steadily drawing away along the canal, and Harry's path was blocked a little way along by a thick hawthorn hedge.

"Tha mun cross over, then, and come along wi'," said the boy. Looking around, Harry saw that a little brick bridge crossed over from the field beside the garden to the towpath, and she scampered back to cross by it quickly, and catch up with the boat again. It was covered thickly with cow pats let drop by the homeward cows from the pasture. Harry splashed through in her button boots, and stained her pinafore as she went. The long satin ribbons on her straw hat slipped loose, and the hat sailed off her head as she jumped off the stile between bridge and towpath. It landed on the water, and floated. The slight wash left by the pair of boats moved it gently sideways till it caught up in a wild-rose bush that overhung the edge of the water. Harry spared it only the briefest glance before deciding that she couldn't reach it back; then she raced along the towpath and caught her sleeve on a thorn, and the fine wool of her dress was ripped into a large hole on her arm.

The boat was moving away smoothly and steadily, and slow though its pace was, she would have had trouble catching up with it, had there not been a lock concealed just around the bend, and that lock, moreover, full when they needed it empty, so that horse and boat and butty boat were all stopped. Harry came up with them with a stitch in her side, and breathless.

The boy was too busy to talk to her. And Harry saw with astonishment that the leading boat was being handled not by a real grownup but by a big girl of about seventeen or so. Harry watched them put cranked brass windlasses onto the winding gear beside the lock, and, leaning and heaving, wind a great toothed iron bar upward, slowly, out of the ground. As they did so, the water at the foot of the lock gate began to churn and boil like a pot of Cook's good brown soup, and the water in the lock began to fall away. A dark deep cleft lined with slimy wet masonry opened in the ground at Harry's feet. In the bottom of it lay water, disturbed by a noisy white jet escaping into it from a leak around the side of the top gate. The boy and girl waited patiently. Then they put their backsides against the great white balance beam that reached across from the top of the lower lock gate, and overhung the path beside it, and began to strain and heave backward against it. It swung slowly away behind them, and the gate opened into a recess in the sides of the lock. There was a similar gate on the side of the lock on which Harry was standing, and while the others were scrambling across the catwalk over the top gates she put her own weight against her balance beam, and walked backward as they had done, and greatly to her surprise, so massive and heavy did the whole contraption look, it moved smoothly and easily open.

The boy stopped halfway across when he saw what she had done, and retreated, without so much as saying thank you. "Yah! Rosie!" he yelled at the horse, which leaned and started forward, and he ran away down the path to jump aboard the leading boat, lift off the towrope that joined her to the butty, and steer her in. It didn't look to Harry as if the boat could possibly fit into the narrow slit at her feet, but it did, just, with an inch to spare either side, and the boy brought her in without touching. And it looked to Harry again as if the boat would not fit; as if it were far too long for the lower gate to close on it, but as the boy came he flung an unwinding coil of rope to the girl, who caught it and dropped a loop of it over a bollard on the lockside, and tugged; and the boat came to a standstill just clear of the lower gates, and just an inch or so before her front end touched the upper ones. Harry watched what would happen next, and as the girl closed one gate behind the boat, she swung on her balance beam and closed the other one.

"Lower the paddle!" yelled the girl, tossing the brass windlass across at Harry.

"I beg your pardon?" said Harry, baffled, and not much liking being bossed around. But the girl had let the windlass her side spin around a dozen turns, had taken it off the iron bar, and was running with it to the similar contraption the other end of the lock.

"Let it run down, see," said the boy from deep below her. He looked up at her from his place at the tiller. "Lift that ratchet, and it'll go. Keep hold, mind —or the windlass'll jump off and clobber you!" Harry lifted the ratchet, and got her fingers covered in thick black grease. The oily bar dropped away rumbling into the ground, and the windless ripped around and around, twisting in her grasp. When it stopped, she dropped the windlass, and nursed an aching wrist; saw her filthy fingers, and wiped them clean on her pinafore before she could stop herself.

"Go git the other one up, then," called the boy.

"Well, really!" said Harry crossly.

"Are ye helping or ain't ye?" said the boy, his bright blue eyes scowling up at her.

So Harry helped. Baffled at first, and not understanding the lock gear, she wound the paddles that filled and emptied locks, and caught the rope, which was both wet and grimy with coal dust, and several times got wound around Harry herself as well as the bollard it was meant for. Once, trying to cross the lock to retrieve a windlass carelessly left lying on

the wrong side, she tried to jump down onto the roof of the cabin, and off again, as she had seen the others do, and she took a tumble through the top cloths, and fell onto the cargo, which was coal. She had never in her life worked so hard, but the locks came quickly one after the other, every hundred yards or so, and each lock had to have the boats worked through it one at a time, and there just didn't seem to be any time to stop and think. Perhaps two hours later they had got both boats up through the last lock in what the boy called "the flight," though if that was flying, Harry muttered to herself, she was sorry for birds. The boy brought away the pair of windlasses from the last gate, and they all sat down for a moment on the cabin roof of the butty boat.

"Do you always have to work so hard?" Harry asked them.

"Only when the bleeding lock keeper's having his bleeding lunch!" said the girl with a sudden grin. Her face and lips were dark with sunburn and coal dust, and her gums looked amazingly pink and glossy when she smiled. Harry was shocked at her swearing, and thought how Susan, or her mother, would blanch at such a word; at the same moment, leaning over, she caught sight of her own reflection in the glassy cloud-filled water.

She was disheveled and filthy from top to toe. It dawned on her that she would be in terrible trouble for getting in such a state, if indeed she wasn't al-

ready in terrible trouble for running off out of the garden, and not being there when they called her in, as they surely might have by now—for the sun was high and hot, and the dew was gone off the thick grass and flowers of the path. And Susan, who might well have hidden away her dirty clothes, and washed and mended them quietly, would not be there to run to.

Harry burst into tears.

"Wa's up wi' ye?" asked the boy. "Ast hurt your arm, winding them old paddles?"

"It's not that," wailed Harry, through her tears.

"That's easily done, that is," said the boy uneasily.

"What is the matter, then?" asked the girl. "For we maun be going onwards, and you'd best get back. And thank you kindly for aiding us along," she added after a pause. Harry kept sobbing.

"Tell us, then," said the boy, gruffly.

Harry said she would get into terrible trouble when they saw how torn and dirty she had got her clothes. Indeed, her tears flowed freely as she thought of it, what with the disgrace she was in already for not liking the new house.

"Where are you from, then?" they asked her.

"The big house back there."

"And don' they treat you kindly?"

"No!" said Harry indignantly. "They don't! I'm so homesick for the other house we've just moved from, and they take no notice of me at all, only to give me work to do, that I must do all by myself, for they're all too busy to help me, and I've spent the last three days locked in a bare room just for not being cheerful, and this morning they turned me out into the garden in the wet morning, and forbade me to come in!"

"It's a wicked shame!" said the girl with sudden passion. "They take childer into big houses, and then they don't find a mite of kindness for them, for all the work they get. Only beatings. Do ye ever get beaten, poor wench? For if ye do, ye'll get another for that torn sleeve."

"Oh, yes, I sometimes do," sobbed Harry. For her governess did use a ruler on her knuckles often enough, and the torn dress would surely mean worse trouble than adding up sums wrong.

"Mrs. Wilkins at Spillers Lock needs a girl, Bess," said the boy, suddenly. "And she's a kind old body. Could we take the lass down to her along of us?"

"Oh, I dunno, Ned," said the girl. "She don't look much of a hand at things. Ma Wilkins wants a good worker."

"Can ye work hard?" asked Ned, looking straight at Harry.

"Certainly I can," said Harry haughtily, for she was filled with sudden relief at the thought of escape, of getting away from the horrid house, and not having to face up to the terrible scene for her spoiled clothes, and although somewhere in a sneaking way she knew that they would be worried about her, she really had no idea how much, and thought it would serve them right for being so harsh with her.

"They'll come after her," said Bess.

"A short way, mebbe," said Ned. "On the roads more like, sooner than herealong. What do they care? They'll just get themselves another girl from somewheres." A slight twinge of fear troubled Harry, for she realized that she would in truth be searched after rather more keenly than the serving girl they had taken her for.

"We could do with a third pair of hands, indeed we could," said Bess. She again looked thoughtfully at Harry.

"Where's the harm?" said Ned.

"Stir theeself then, Ned, we'd best keep moving," said Bess suddenly.

"Gerrup, Rosie!" yelled Ned at the horse, twitching the towrope, and the horse shook her flanks, and leaned, and very slowly the boats began to glide forward, and Ned leaned on the great upturned multicolored tiller and swung the butty boat *Beatrice* out into mid-channel behind the *Mary*.

Harry sat in the sun on the cabin roof of the butty and chatted to Ned, watching Bess, in the boat ahead, steer with effortless skill against the sideways pull of the towrope toward the towpath bank. Bess wore a frilled white bonnet, with a flounce hanging down to keep the sun off her neck, and Harry had not been mistaken, for the horse Rosie was wearing a bonnet too, of white crochet work. Ned said it was to keep the flies out of her ears.

Ned told Harry about Mrs. Wilkins, a widow, whose husband had been the keeper of Spillers Lock, and how the canal company had let Mrs. Wilkins stay on and take over her husband's duties, and how she needed someone willing and spry to help her open and close gates and collect the toll money, and keep the kettle boiling for her cups of tea.

At length Ned let Harry try the tiller, with his hand on it beside her own while she got used to it, for you had to thrust it to the right to turn the boat's front leftward, and left to swing right, like doing something in a mirror. The butty boat followed the course of the lead boat, and you had to steer clear down the middle of the canal—Ned called it "the cut"—and go around the outer side of any bend.

Harry was enchanted. She kept her eye fixed on the *Mary* and felt the long length of the *Beatrice* respond to her pressure on the tiller, slowly and smoothly. Ned instructed her on watching ahead. Along a straight reach, the butty boat was drawn smoothly along behind the lead boat, but on a bend the butty had to steer its own course toward the outer bank, resisting the pull of the connecting rope as the lead boat turned.

Harry was learning nicely, until, as they came around a sharp corner, she suddenly saw coming

toward Rosie on the towpath another horse, and behind it, remorselessly gliding toward them, the front
of another pair of boats, going the other way. "Oh,
Ned!" she cried.

"Hold right, Harry, hold right," he said calmly, taking the tiller from her. Harry watched.

"They're unladen, so they pass over us," said Ned.

"Pass over?" said Harry, baffled. But the boy who
was leading the horse coming toward them led his
horse between Rosie and the hedge, and as the two
horses passed, pulled the bridle. His horse stopped
for a mere moment, his towrope slackened, and he
lifted it over Rosie's back. Then his horse tugged
again, and the rope came rapidly across the *Mary*,
high, because of the height of the towing posts.

To Harry's astonishment, the chimney on the
Mary's cabin bent before it, so the rope swept on
toward them. Ned, reaching up, flipped a latch on
their own chimney, bent it double, ducked grace-
fully under the rope as it passed him, and set the
chimney up again. He nodded to the man at the
tiller of the other pair. He hadn't taken his eyes off
the curve of the cut ahead of them, or stopped steer-
ing for a moment. Harry soon discovered why he was
so easy at it, for it happened again and again all
afternoon, as boats passed them working the other
way. Ned said there were just as many boats going
the same way as they, but they would see these only
when they were stopped at a lock, or tied up resting,

for they all moved at much the same speed, and were spaced out along the distance like beads on a string.

The sun baked down on them, and there were birds and water rats to look at, and when they felt thirsty Ned fetched a brightly painted ladle covered in roses, which he called "the dipper," and plunged it in the painted jug which stood on the roof beside the chimney, and the water came to their lips warm and slightly tinny. Once or twice they came to another lock, and real work began again. The three of them worked the boats, and one side of the lock, while the keeper worked the other. It was much easier than the locks they had come through without help at lunch time, but Bess and Ned were very jumpy and nervous at them just the same. "What's the matter, Ned?" asked Harry, wondering with a twitch of fear if perhaps he was afraid that the lock keeper would guess she was a runaway, and start a hue and cry. "Nowt," said Ned, glaring at her ferociously.

By the late afternoon, Harry was very tired. She could hardly lift her feet from the ground, and became clumsy at jumping back onto the boat as it left the locks. Twice she put a foot in the water, nearly falling in. A sort of inner clock inside her kept expecting Susan or her governess to come and take her home. But nobody came. Bess brought a painted nose pan of oats, and hung it on Rosie's bridle. Harry won-

dered why she had not been followed. The boats were not moving very fast, and they could easily have been caught up with. Obviously now Susan had gone, nobody cared. The day wore on into a long, tranquil green evening, and the boats still moved steadily onward. The water below them grew all shiny with the low slope of the light; the air became cooler and full of shadows. The sky began to rainbow with watery sunset shades, while a few streaky clouds high above them still caught the sun, and shone silver, weaving ribbons of brightness in the mirrored depths. Clouds of insects hung over the water. Harry got bitten.

At last, when it was nearly dark, they came to a lock with a cottage and a pub, and stables beside it, and here they tied up for the night. The horse was unharnessed, and groomed, Ned brushing the lower parts, legs and flanks, which he could reach from the ground, and Bess on a stool dealing with the horse's back and shoulders. Rosie was an enormous Shire horse, with great plumes of hair around her hoofs which took Ned a while to comb out clean of burrs and mud cakes, but he wouldn't let Harry help because Rosie didn't know her touch, and might get restive. When Rosie was safely stalled for the night, Ned fetched a jug of brown ale from the inn and they retired for supper to the cabin of the *Mary*. The cabin on the butty was not being used this trip, Ned said, there being so few of them.

Inside, the cabin was like Harry's dollhouse, so small and neat and bright it was. Across the back was a wide bed over a cupboard, with lacy curtains hanging across it. Down the right-hand side of the cabin ran a bench, which made a "side bed" at night, and seating by day, and on the left side was a stove and cooking range, with a big brass rail around it to stop the kettle sliding off the hob, and rails over it to dry clothes on. A huge copper kettle shared the top of the stove with a black iron stewpot. Between the stove and the bed stood a cupboard with a prettily painted door, shaped like a church window, and hinged at the bottom, so that the door let down to make a table when they sat to eat, and inside the cupboard was food; there was bread and cheese, and a clutch of moor hen's eggs that Ned had picked up that morning, and a copper caddy of tea. Spoons and forks lived in a little drawer below the table-top door, and below that was another cupboard. Even the step by which they came down from the deck outside was the coalbox in disguise. Every inch of cabin wall was covered with lace-edged plates, threaded with ribbon like fairground prizes, or with straps and hooks for hanging odds and ends upon; and the only movable objects in the whole tight little place apart from cooking vessels were a painted stool and the oil lamp that cast so warm a glow on all the sparkling brass and copper.

Bess served them with soup from the iron pot, and

broke an egg into each steaming bowlful. Ned broke
hunks off the lump of bread, and they sat and ate
from battered tinware spoons, too hungry to speak a
word till the bowls were empty and scraped almost
clean.

"Is there more, Bess?" asked Ned.

Harry was glad he asked, for she wouldn't have
liked to herself.

"Soup yes, bread no, or there'll be nowt for
morning," said Bess.

Harry began to drowse in the warmth, and yawn and nod.

"Out wi' you, then, young Ned," said Bess briskly.

"Not for long, Bess. I'm cold and spent."

"Sooner you go, sooner you can come back," said Bess, shutting him out. She poured water from the warm kettle into a bowl, and offered it to Harry to wash. Harry, who had hardly ever had to wash herself without Susan to help her, and never without a large basin of water and mounds of clean soft towels, did her best, but it was not good enough for Bess, who took over and scrubbed Harry's neck and arms and hands with a flannel rag, till Harry glowed, and then began on herself with equal vigor. Harry noticed with a twinge of shame that Bess, though she had probably never had more than a pint of water a day to wash in, and had spent the day since Harry met her in just the same way as Harry, had not got nearly so dirty. Just the same, when she had removed all but her underwear, and taken off her flounced bonnet, and cleaned her face, she looked much younger, so that Harry, who had taken her for nearly grownup—for quite a young woman—was startled, and suddenly more afraid.

"How old are you, Bess?" she asked.

"Fourteen, far as I know," said Bess.

"Aren't you too young to manage a boat on your own?" said Harry.

"Yes, daresay I am. Wouldn't be allowed on a

company boat, not till the skipper's twenty-one. I never done it before, and won't be let again in a hurry, even if we do get down in time."

Harry would have gone on asking, but at that point Bess had finished washing. She poured clean water for Ned, and laid out a towel for him, and then she came and lay down on the bed with Harry, and drew the curtains across, and, reaching up, knocked smartly on the cabin roof. Ned came in from the cold outside, and Harry could hear him splashing his bowl of water, and then emptying the slops outside.

When he had finished they drew the bed curtain again, and Harry saw him lying on the side bench, with his jacket rolled up under his head for a pillow. She felt suddenly terribly crowded and alone. She longed for her wide soft bed in the empty nursery of the old familiar house, and she felt like pushing Bess off the bed, or lashing out at the brown, sharp-eyed strange faces so oppressively near her. Nothing had ever been allowed to happen to Harry; she was never allowed out of sight for long, never allowed to run or climb in case she hurt herself, was kept from being frightened, kept from being uncomfortable, always fetched home by bedtime. She simply couldn't believe this could be happening—were they *really* not going to find her, not going to come and take her home, and scold her, and put her safely to sleep in a wide soft bed by herself? She choked back a sob, and turned over to face the wooden wall, shuddering to think of all that great weight of coal the other side of a few planks, only inches from her nose, and pretended to fall asleep. In a little while Bess put out the lamp.

The boat was not quite still. Harry couldn't *feel* it rocking, on the smooth water, but it somehow seemed softly afloat—not quite solid. And it wasn't quite quiet either; there were odd creakings, and faint watery noises from outside, and little tappings on the hull and the splash of a water rat venturing out. Harry was very warm now, under a crochet cover, and close against Bess, and she ached a good deal from working so hard. Tiredness weighed down on her like a great load within her head, but she was so unused to the murmurings and shiftings going on around her that she couldn't quite sleep at once, and so by and by she heard Ned saying in a soft, urgent voice, "Shall we make it, Bess, d'ye think?"

"I dunno, Ned, truly. But we mebbe shall."

"We've another pair of hands to the locks now."

"And did we do right, I wonder?"

"We could do with the help, Bess. How'd we have gone along so well today, if we hadn't have found her?"

"That's right enough," said Bess.

"Well, so. We'm in the lurch, and we gotta find help. And Ma Wilkins could do with a girl."

"I'd be easier if she weren't so pretty spoken, or if

she seemed used to showing herself handy. If she'd noticed when the fire needed mending, or summat. And, Ned, when we were washing, I saw not a mark on her."

"You fret too much, Bess," said Ned. "Why would she come along wi' us except she weren't happy?"

And Harry lay there listening, really very frightened, and vowing to be handier at mending the fire and such like, and to take care to seem like a servant girl. For if it would have been bad enough to go back dirty at lunch time, it would be terrible—Harry couldn't even begin to imagine how bad—to go back after spending the whole night away, and so, clearly, she would just have to be a serving girl now, and work for Mrs. Wilkins. The only trouble was, Harry had never taken the least notice of the servants except for Susan.

Still, she managed better the next day. It got easier as she got used to it. The boats could only travel each day as far as the horse could manage; the horse was considered first in every way. They filled her painted nose pan, gave her water, checked her hoofs for stones every few miles, groomed her, made sure her harness did not chafe, cherished her in every way possible. Harry was awestruck at the sight of Ned's small form, bent over, holding across his crooked knees the enormous hoofs of Rosie, with their flowing plumes of hair, looking for stones between shoe and hoof. Rosie took it calmly enough, though she had a tendency to start to lean against Ned. "Gerroff!" he would yell at her, just before she pushed him into the cut. When they came to a lock, it was the custom for the boat crew to work one side, while the lock keeper worked the other, and Harry soon got used to playing her part in this. But between locks she could sit on the butty cabin roof, one hand on the tiller, watching England winding slowly by, full of pleasant sights, fields and churches and raw new railway cuttings, and streams and farmhouses. More often she would trot alongside Rosie, urging her on, and chatting to her, and seeing the wild flowers thickly clustered by the water's edge, many of them unknown to Harry, who had never known a marshy place before. As she went she spotted moor hens' nests in the reeds, or startled rabbits, but she quickly learned not to tell Ned about nests because he stole the eggs at once for their supper, and, oddly, Harry felt painfully sorry for the mother birds, returning to their empty homes. He found enough without her, anyway.

Sometimes she helped Bess on the lead boat, putting coal on the fire, and various things in the stewpot toward supper. Some of the things that went into that pot were lifted from canal-side fields or gardens, and once there was a rabbit Ned hit with his catapult, and several times there were fish, from lines Ned set in the evening. Ned was the first boy Harry had ever spent much time with, for the children invited to play with her at home had always been other little girls. She thought he was splendid, with his stocky toughness, and his cleverness at catching things, and his bright cheerful eyes.

When they passed a shop on the towpath they would spend a few pence on provisions, but even with Harry's pocket money, which had been in her apron pocket, by good luck, there was very little to spend. Turnip broth was all they ate on more than one occasion. Just the same, Harry looked forward enormously to supper. She began to think food was really one of the very best things in the world; she had never in her life before been hungry enough to enjoy it. Polishing brassware in the cabin and shining the plates was girls' work, but it was Ned's job to clean the brass bands on the chimney pot and swab down the painted cabins, and the boats' names, *Mary* and *Beatrice*, on the front ends.

Harry soon learned to call the canal "the cut," and the reaches between one lock and the next "pounds," and herself, casual worker as she was, a "huffler." She learned too the serious side of things and some of the meaning of the conversation she had heard between Ned and Bess on that first night. The Jebb family had a contract with a paper mill to bring down coal from the mines; Ned and Bess's father was a "number one," which meant he owned his own boats, and worked as his own master, supplying the paper mill. *Mary* and *Beatrice* were a pair he had bought for his eldest son, Tom, to start up with.

"Tom's been waiting four year for a contract wi' the mill," Ned told Harry. "There's always more number ones wanting work than the mill owner can do wi', so he keeps a list of men with good boats ready. And Tom's name no sooner come to the top, than he broke his arm, back up at the mine, loading his first cargo; and we maun get his coal down to the mill, or they'll give his contract to the next man on their list. And he'll be in trouble if we'm late with it too, that's why we'm pressed and fretful about the time we'm making."

"Rosie's a good horse," said Bess. "She'll go on mile after mile with just the odd crack of the whip from the boats to keep her at it. But we go much faster and safer when she's led along."

"It was lucky both ways we met you," said Ned.

"Please, Ned," Harry said, "I know I'm not used to any of this, but I'll do my best to help you more, if you'll just tell me how."

"You do well enough, for a lass, Harry," Ned said, quietly. "You got the hang of the tiller quicker'n what I did, that was born in a butty."

They all had enough to worry about, in fact. Harry knew there must be a search for her going on; Bess and Ned had Tom's cargo date on their minds; all three were jumpy lest someone should notice that there were three children handling a pair of boats without an adult. But many of the other boats they passed had families on board, and children at the tillers or leading the horses; so that just the sight of children working the boats caused no remark.

At one lock, though, the lock keeper was talking to a canal company inspector as they worked through.

"Where's your number one?" they asked Harry, as the water lowered her past their feet into the lock chamber.

"Down below, getting some sleep," said Harry unflinchingly. "We were working late yesterday."

"Did you hear that, Bess?" said Ned admiringly, as soon as they drew out of earshot. "That was dead artful, Harry. And you never even blinked. Good on you!"

Bess said darkly, "Yes, Ned, I heard her. She lies as fast as a dog can lick a dish, don't she?"

But even then their worries seemed very dream-like and unreal to Harry. They couldn't exactly hurry; they went as fast as Rosie could pull, and could go no faster. And time simply wore away in a kind of hard-working tranquillity.

Just now and then Harry was overcome with attacks of homesickness. Once Ned saw the look on her face, and asked her if she was thinking about the big house, and Harry said yes. And Ned took her hand, and said to her very softly and kindly, "You put all that far behind you, little Harry. The world's a wide place, and you need never see that house again, nor anyone from it evermore get sight or sound of you."

And at that, of course, Harry felt worse, though she tried bravely to smile at him.

Then that night, when the cabin doors were closed and bolted, and the three of them were lying snugly in the dark, Harry couldn't help crying. Ned didn't stir, but Bess, who was lying so close to Harry, woke up and said sleepily, "What's up wi' thee, then?"

"Oh, nothing, Bess," said Harry, choking as she tried to swallow her sobs. "I'm sorry I woke you."

"Don't you like it on the cut, maybe?" whispered Bess. "Is it too hard for you?"

"Oh, no," said Harry. "I love it. And you are so kind to me."

"You running off from a hard place, and you liking it with us, then," said Bess. "There oughtern't to be much to weep for."

"I'm missing Susan," said Harry, with her eyes brimming again. "She was always good to me, and we had little jokes and secrets together. If they hadn't sent Susan away, I don't think I would have run off . . ."

"Who's Susan?" asked Bess.

"The nurserymaid."

"Ah. However bad things get, like can always stick by like," said Bess. "That's what my ma says." Harry didn't really understand that, but she was already nearly asleep, on her damp pillow.

They had been going four long days when they met real trouble. All one morning they met no boats coming the other way, as Ned uneasily re-marked, more than once. Then they came around a bend in the cut, leading to the next lock, and found a long line of boats tied up, and others jamming the mid-channel, and men and horses thronging the towpath. Some way ahead they could see the lock; across it a pair of shear legs made of tree trunks made a wigwam-shaped outline against the sky.

"Oh, no!" said Ned between his teeth. And they steered in to the towpath, knocked in their mooring pins, and tied up, the butty abreast of the leading boat.

"Better run up there, an' see what's wrong, Ned," said Bess. "And we'll go below and stay there. Some-one's gonna see we're alone!" The two girls cowered in the cabin, with the doors shut. In a while Ned came back, nearly crying. "Some bleeding cock-brains have silled their butty, and broken her back in the lock, while they were drinking in the inn," he said.

"Oh gawd," said Bess.

"What's it mean? What's 'silled'?" asked Harry.

"It's letting the back of the boat lie over the ledge below the top gates, when the lock is draining out," said Ned. "The back of the boat gets left high and dry on the sill, while the rest goes on down with the water, and the weight of the cargo has bust the bleeding boat. There's men down in the lock, cutting it up, and them shear legs ready to lift it out. All day!

All day it will take, Bess! And the whole place crawling with canal company men to look cutty-eyed at us!"

"Whatta we gonna do, Ned?" said Bess helplessly. And just at that moment there came a smart rap on the cabin side, and a man's voice calling.

Very slowly Bess stood up, slid back the hatch, and stood up into view. "Where's Tom Jebb, then, girl?" said the voice outside. "These are his boats, aren't they? Tell him look sharp and lively, and go give his name to the lock keeper. There's one pair of boats shoved ahead of him already, and he'll lose his place, an' miss his turn if he ain't careful."

"Can't we just wait here, then?" asked Bess, in a shaky voice.

"You'll wait a week if you do. There's been men fighting up there already about who's to be first through when it's clear, and the constable called out to part them. The lock keeper is making a list of who come when, and that's the order we'll go through in. He better get along there quick. You just tell him. Why, what's up, girl, 'tain't the end of the world!"

"You a friend of Tom's, mister?" said Bess.

"Couldn't really say that," said the voice outside. "I know 'im. I ain't his enemy."

"He broke his arm, see," said Bess. "He ain't here."

"Who's in charge, then?" said the voice.

"Me," said Bess. "You won't tell on us, mister, will ye?"

"You and who else?" said the man. Bess opened the cabin door, and he looked inside.

"We gotta keep his contract date," said Ned. "It's his first run."

"Ah," said the stranger. He was a tough-looking blond man in his mid-forties. He wore a wide leather belt with a boatman's windlass in it. "You're in a spot, then, aren't you? Tell you what I'll do. I'll go put your name down. Or Tom's, rather. Anyone else bothers you, you tell 'em Tom's gone off for an hour or two. We'll be just ahead of you, so when we get through I'll send my big boy to work your pair past the lock; he looks grown man enough. But meanwhile, don't you stay shut in here; a closed-up boat will make people wonder; you sit out on the cabin like you hadn't a care in the world. Right, then?"

"Oh, *thank you!*" cried Harry. "You are kind!"

"Oh, Tom'll do summat for me, sometime, don't doubt," said the stranger, moving off.

So they emerged and sat in the sun. Just in front of them a butty was tied up, with a woman sitting in the cabin door, cradling a baby and humming to it. Little groups of men chatted together on the towpath. Time wore on. Harry and Ned went twice to look at the work in the lock. The broken boat had been sawn apart. A false stern was being fixed across the end of her hold, to float her away, and the shear legs were being used to lift out the cabin section.

A great press of people stood around watching. Ned

and Harry felt uneasy in the crowd, so they didn't linger there, but returned to the boats. They were no longer at the back of the line; more boats had come up behind them, and still more came, every half hour or so, till the towpath was crowded for a mile or so back from the lock. The boatmen came up along the towpath, asking what was amiss, and cursing when they heard.

Harry skipped lightly across the front ends and back ends, and along the narrow toehold of the gunwale all around the boats, playing catch with Ned, while Bess, sitting drowsing in the sun, leaning against the cabin door, grunted in annoyance as they brushed past her. Light-footed and cocksure, Harry ran down the line of planks laid amidships over the coal, and suddenly slipped, and rolled down the sloping side cloths over the side into the water. She came up gasping, clutched at the smooth slippery sides of the *Mary*'s hull, screamed, and went under again. When she surfaced a second time, a stout man was leaning out from the *Mary*, reaching a hand to her, and Ned, white-faced, was holding the boat's shaft, which he had hooked into her dress to pull her in by.

"Don't, Ned, you'll tear it!" she said, spluttering and choking.

"Vanity at death's door!" said the man, getting a firm hold of Harry's hand. "Blooming women." And he pulled her out, and set her, dripping, on the cabin roof. "You want to be more careful, young scamp," he said. "You can drown in the cut as quick as in the ocean. Lucky I was near, that's what. You wouldn't be cavorting about on the boats like that if your number one were in sight, I'll bet." At the mention of the nonexistent number one they must all have looked scared, for he went on, "You may well look woeful. Drowning's no joke. Just two days ago we come past a spot where they were dragging the cut for a young lady. All they could find was her hat."

"Heavens, Harry!" exclaimed Bess. "You're shaking like you had a winter wetting. You come and get outer them wet clothes at once!"

As the afternoon wore on, Harry lay in the cabin, while her clothes dried out hanging over the stove, and Ned wandered on the towpath, keeping an eye on the work at the lock.

"You might as well take a kip, Harry," said Bess. "We won't be to bed early tonight." And it was very hot and sleepy in the cabin, with the sun beating down on its roof and wooden side, and the fire crackling quietly in the stove. Harry put her head down, and drifted to sleep.

She was wakened by a sound of shouting a little distance off. The lock had been cleared, and the crowd was cheering. "Git your clothes on, then," said Bess. "We'll be moving shortly."

Harry put on her petticoats, very scratchy to her skin, for they had dried stiff in the heat, and her woolen dress, with the hole in the sleeve getting worse, and her pinafore. Her boots were hanging upside down over the kettle, and they too were stiff and hard to get on. When at last she was laced and buttoned up, and she put her head out of the cabin hatch, she was surprised to see that it was nearly dusk. The trees cast long shadows, the sky was rosy pink behind the wheat field across the cut. The idle crowds on the towpath had become silent and busy; the horses were being harnessed up, the pins drawn, and the boats moved up toward the lock. Harry saw in the distance the lock gates open to reveal a pair of boats. They began to move down the cut toward her, their towrope passing over the roofs of the waiting line of boats. It took a long time for the *Mary* and *Beatrice* to reach the head of the line. It was very nearly dark when they were suddenly joined by the big boy whose help they had been promised, and they worked through the lock at last. Above the lock, many of the boats were tied up while the boatmen took their supper, and little disks of golden light shone from the lamplit cabins, and were echoed in the dark water. The shadowy shapes of bushes overhung the towpath, and cast everything into darkness, and there were voices in the gloom, and horses snorting and stamping while they were settled for the night. Bess and Ned took their boats up to the head of the moored line, and tied up there.

"I've only just got dressed," Harry complained. "And I'll have to undress again right away."

"Don't fear that," said Bess. "We'll stop and sup till the moon gets up, and then we go on. You'll have your clothes on awhile yet."

"*Can* we move in the dark?" asked Harry, astonished.

"Can if we must," said Ned. "Rosie done no work today, so she'll have some pull left in her. An' we maun git down to Mill Lock by today, or we'll not make Tom's date. Can you manage, Harry, do ye think?"

"*I'm* all right," said Harry stoutly. "I had a sleep this afternoon."

"We'm all right, likewise," he said. " 'Twon't be the first time we've moonlighted, nor the last."

So after supper the hatch was opened again, and they sat looking up at the square of black velvet pricked with stars that it left in the cabin roof, waiting for moonrise.

"We don't have any luck, when you come to think of it," said Bess, mournfully.

"Oh, I don' know so much," said Ned. "Could have happened at new moon, Bess, or in clouded weather. Or we could have missed meeting Harry."

When at last the moon was up and in sight over the sloping fields, the children climbed out into the air again.

"Shan't I bring the lamp?" asked Harry.

"No, no," said Ned. "It would blind us with brightness. We need to be owl-eyed. Just wait till your eyes open up to the gloom."

Ned was right. What seemed at first to be inky blackness outside gradually took shape as a dark picture, like a very black woodcut in one of Harry's storybooks. A pale frost of light lay over the silent land. The humps of hills, the treetops, the parapet of the next bridge over the cut, every upper side where a dusting of snow might lie in winter was frozen silver. A thin glaze of translucent sheen like paper-thin ice covered the surface of the canal. But every hollow, every lower growth, the bridge hole, the places where the hedge leaned over the towpath or the sedges of the water's edge leaned over the water, were cast into a soft blackness as thick as nightmare. As the boats moved gently onward, the surface of the water beneath them broke into dishes of pale light, rocking on an oily blackness, as globules of moonlight floated on the troubled surface; behind them, when Harry looked back, the water was black, black, with only a dying line of moon-silvered wash trailing out. Yet they could see perfectly all they needed. They could steer down mid-channel as well as in daylight, except for one short stretch where trees leaned over the water on both sides, and threw a tunnel of moonshadow across them. They passed a village with silver roofs, and a shining church spire, a ghost gloss on the cobbled street beside the cut, and only one upper window lit, warm and gold. They passed a wide mile of farm land, with a ghost harvest on it, all of silver wheat, and a faint farmhouse where a dog barked crisp and clear across the silence. The locks were easy to see, their white painted balance beams showed clearly; but the lock chambers were so dark and deep as the boats sank into them that Harry almost cried with fright, shuddering and looking up at the stars for comfort, and sighing with relief as the gates were swung back, and ahead of her again she could see the moonshine route of the next pound. The lock keepers were very cheerful and friendly, though it was so late; Bess said they were paid extra for nightwork. And so they went on and on.

By the time they reached the Mill Lock they were like ghosts themselves, in their ghost landscape. They had long since fallen silent from weariness, and moved slowly, with heavy limbs. They had white faces, with deep black-shadowed eye sockets, and shining hair. Just before the moon went down they tied up the boat, and tethered Rosie where she could crop the towpath grass, and lay down unwashed and still dressed in the cabin, to instant sleep.

It was noon the next day, when they were still rather tired and cross from losing so much sleep, that Rosie cast a shoe. Harry was at the tiller of the butty when it happened, and she had to bring the boat into the bank, and tie it up before she could run up to join the other two and see what had happened.

They were standing with stricken faces, talking urgently. Ned was holding the worn shoe.

"We'll have to take Rosie on or back, and then come back to the boats, Ned." Bess was saying. "Either way we'll lose best part of a day. It's ten mile back to the smithy at Ponders Lock, and maybe even farther to the next one on. Face it, Ned," she said. "We're not going to make it now. 'Tisn't our fault."

"It's mine!" cried Ned, almost weeping. "I muster missed a worn nail when I checked her hoofs last night. But I did look, Bess, honest I did!"

"What's wrong with the blacksmith back there?" asked Harry.

"Back where?" asked Bess blankly.

"Just a quarter mile back, in the village we just came through."

"There ain't no blacksmith there, Harry. We'd know."

"He's new . . ." Harry began.

"We'd best get trudging back along," said Bess wearily. "I'm sorry, Ned, honest I am, but we just ain't going to make it. I never promised. I only said we'd try."

"But there *is* a blacksmith," said Harry, almost stamping. "Two hundred yards up the street from the bridge. 'Newly established. All classes of work undertaken.' So don't worry, Ned, it's not far."

"Now, how would you know a thing like that,

Harry?" said Bess, suddenly looking at her hard.

"There's a notice on the bridge, saying so, silly," said Harry, "in letters a yard high. Didn't you see it?"

But they both gaped at her. "Where did you learn to read, then?" said Bess, with a rather desperate note in her voice.

Harry realized too late that she had given herself away again. "Sunday school," she said bravely. "I used to go to Sunday school."

"I got enough on my mind," said Bess miserably, "without fretting over who you are, or where you come from."

"There's a Sunday school in almost every village," said Harry hopefully, as though defending her fib.

"*I* wouldn't mind knowing how to read," said Ned. "Comes in handy, times like now. Come on, then, let's get the old hoss to the smith."

And indeed there was a blacksmith, just where Harry said one would be, and he put a new set of shoes on Rosie within the hour for eighteen pence, which Bess paid him out of an oilskin bag from a drawer in the cabin ceiling which she called the monkey box. And while they waited, the blacksmith's wife gave them a little round apple pasty each, hot from the oven.

On the fifth day the canal went through a town. First, very close beside the cut, was a foundry—a great tall building with a towering black chimney from which smoke poured, and lay across the sky like a thundercloud; within the upper windows of this building fire could be seen, and on the desolate ground outside it heaps of coal were piled. A narrowboat tied up at its wharf was being unloaded by three men with shovels. A smell of acrid and sulphurous air hung around them, and a racket of roaring flame and grinding machinery came from the blackened walls beyond.

Harry shuddered at this place, but Ned told her she would be hard put to it to get by without using iron. "Nails and stoves and saucepans, Harry, wheels and hammers and windlass gear, flatirons and horseshoes, and coal-hole covers, and pipes and boilers and buckets and chains; there's folks laboring making iron for all of that, Harry, working all their lives in that building, not just roving past it!"

Beyond the foundry the canal bank began to be lined either side at a little distance by street ends of mean, close-packed houses, and yards and sheds and wharves. The water in the cut was black and opaque, slickened with a treacly foulness. But the countryside came with them in an ever-narrowing column, infiltrating beside the water, a slender band of grasses and valiant flowers, a little long acre of wasteland like neglected meadow in the heart of the stony town. Great warehouses of sore red brick grimed with soot towered over the canal banks, and soon closed in on them from either side, till Rosie trod a narrow ledge at the foot of a cliff of hideous wall, and the boats swam behind her in a dark deep cleft, under a mere ribbon of distant sky, on water that lay in shadow from dawn to dusk. At length the sinister wall to the right and the sinister wall to the left closed right round the canal like a clenched fist; they met and the canal disappeared into a dark hole under a blackened arch beneath. For a few moments Harry could see nothing in the gloom, and then she could just make out a pair of lock gates embedded in the darkness in the bowels of the black building. As they entered it, a band of dirty gray light crossed the

boats; they came under not only the building but the wide low arch of a bridge into the lock. Not more than a foot of daylight fell between tunnel and bridge arch. It was a deep lock, maybe twelve or fourteen feet of slimy blackened lock wall dripping above them as they lay in the bottom of it. Then Ned raised the paddles, and the water began to boil and roll under them, raising them up out of the ground slowly and steadily and as lightly as though both boats and all their cargo were a pair of leaves floating.

Up they came, past the wet masonry of the lock,

and into the sweet sun and air again, and found themselves in the middle of a handsome town, with green public gardens, and a fine tall church with a spire, and wide streets thronging with people. The bridge from under which they had come carried the London road on its way, loud with rolling carriage wheels, and the terrible buildings were chopped down to half height from this higher level, and masked by a row of shops standing in front of them. And from there the canal bent away leftward, past handsome houses with gardens, and in hardly any time at all it was out in the grassy fields again, bringing with it still its trailing ribbon of grassy bank, that had threaded the town through from side to side. Ribbons, Ned said, and gloves and carpets were what those townfolk made for their livelihoods, for the most part. Ned seemed to know a lot about such things.

And after the dark town, as the afternoon wore on, Ned and Bess became brighter and brighter, and laughed and called to each other and to Harry very merrily as they went about their tasks, or stood at the tillers, and with each lock they worked through they became lighter-hearted and more chirpy than before, till Bess was almost skipping and dancing at Rosie's side, and Harry guessed—of course—that they were nearly at the paper mill, and the burden that had gone off her companions like cloudshadow off the countryside was the fear of missing Tom's con-

tract. As for herself, her own secret troubles seemed heavier than ever, but she tried to smile back at Ned.

At last when it grew dark they tied up beside a little cottage inn, and Bess set a supperpot on the fire, and said, "Let's have a tune, Ned, while it heats through," and Ned went down on his knees, and brought out from the chest under the side bed a little painted thing like a pair of wooden platters with a bellows between, from which he squeezed a merry tune, with a fairground sort of sound to it. Harry was entranced, and the accordion brought a group of other boatmen out upon the lawn beside the inn with their beer mugs in their hands, who joined in the singing in a pleasant fashion and repaid Ned by buying the children a jug of ale to wash their dinner down. Harry didn't know any of the songs they sang, which were all about commerce and the arts, and toys made in Birmingham, and the Duke of Bridge-water. But Bess turned out to have a sweet and pretty voice that Harry liked to listen to.

And so they slept like birds in the nest that night, curled up happily in the cabin, and did not move till an hour after daylight, and even so reached the paper mill wharf by eleven the next morning, and found the Jebb parents, with their own pair of boats, waiting there for them.

Ned and Bess brought the *Mary* and the *Beatrice* expertly up alongside *Hope* and *Friendship*, two fine boats, nicely van-dyked, with "w. JEBB AND SONS,

OWNERS, CANAL COAL HAULIERS" in swaggered letters on their cabin sides. A rosy-faced plump woman, her head enveloped in an enormous frilly bonnet, came bobbing up through the cabin hatch on *Friendship,* and said, "Hello, loves," to Ned, and "Where's Tom, then?"

There followed the most tremendous hullabaloo. A trio of smaller Jebb children, whose very existence had not yet been mentioned to Harry, crawled all over the cabin roofs, attacking Bess and Ned with enormous hugs, and mock punches, and shouting joyfully; Bess began upon the tale of Tom's broken arm, whereupon Mrs. Jebb plied her with questions about how bad he was in pain, and Mr. Jebb with questions about how long he would be laid up, likely, and the uproar and talking went on and on, only half understood by Harry, who stayed nearly out of sight in the cabin door of *Mary,* saying nothing. At last, "So who did he get to bring his boats down?" said Mr. Jebb, looking around for some nonexistent person.

"He couldn't find nobody, Da," said Bess. "Though he did try."

"The surgeon said he'd best stay up there, where he could have an eye kept on him," said Ned.

"Didn't seem nothing for it, but to bring the load down on our own, Da," said Bess apologetically. "We done the best we could think of, so don't be angered."

"You'm telling me," said Mr. Jebb, putting his enormous arms akimbo and leaning over his children

from his six-foot height, "that you've come down from the colliery by yourselven, and no trouble on the way?"

"We did have a spot of help," said Ned. "We got a huffler along, sort of."

". . . a servant girl, Da," said Bess, "running off from a harsh position, and we thought Ma Wilkins might take her, for she's handy enough, and willing, and pretty spoken."

"Let's have a look at you, then, little wench," said Mr. Jebb, kindly enough, to Harry, who came slowly out of the cabin of *Mary* and stood trembling and shy before him. "Don't be afraid. We owe you something if you've helped my pair of scamps in doing so well for us," and he smiled at her, from eyes as brightly blue as Ned's, so that she liked him at once, in spite of his bristly chin and rough clothes.

But Mrs. Jebb said, "Mercy, Bess, that ain't no serving girl! That's the child of gentlefolk! What have you done, girl, what have you let us in for!"

"She *said* she was a servant girl!" cried Bess. "Go on, Harry, tell them—tell them what you told us about being locked in and locked out, and beaten!"

Harry blushed, and looked down, away from the circle of accusing eyes.

"She can't tell us, for it ain't true," said Mrs. Jebb, grimly. "Look at her boots, Bess; did you ever see a servant girl wear boots like those? And look at the lace on her pinafore. Oh, Bess, you oughter've known!"

"I wondered how come she could read," muttered Bess miserably.

"*Did* you tell my children that you were an ill-used serving girl?" demanded Mr. Jebb, with real severity.

"Not . . . not exactly . . ." stammered Harry. "I just let them think it, let them go on thinking it once they began to. I did say I had been locked out in the garden . . . and that was *true!* My father thought I looked pale . . ."

"Well, you don't look pale now, girl," said Mrs. Jebb. "Come, William, anyone could see she's come to no harm through us."

"It would be prison for taking a child, Ma," said Mr. Jebb.

"We won't get copped if we just take her to Ma Wilkins," said Ned, hesitantly.

"Or leave her by the cut-side somewhere lonely, and make off in a hurry," said one of the small children. Harry began to cry.

"We'll take her back where she come from," said Mrs. Jebb. "That's all we can do. Now, stop crying, girl. We've got coal to unload, and our journeys to make. But we'll be past your house again within the month, and we'll put you off there. Maybe we won't get caught red-handed with you if we're careful."

"We'll take her back straight away, Ma," said Mr.

Jebb. "That's what we'll do. Tomorrow's Sunday, and I'm not starting to move my boats on Sunday, or half the folk on the cut will wonder what's up wi' me; but first thing Monday we'll go right back the way Tom's pair came down, and we'll have her home in three days or so, with luck."

"You'll miss the next week's cargo, going that way, William Jebb. And what will we eat, may I ask?"

"Bread and drippings for a week or two, I dare-say," he said, frowning. "We've come through that before now, Ma."

"Even that will be hard to come by, with a whole cargo gone missing," said Mrs. Jebb. "And we need a new towrope, bad, Will."

"I'll pawn me watch chain," he said. "We'll eat that."

"And all for a flighty, selfish, lying child . . ." Mrs. Jebb exclaimed. Ned's arm came suddenly around Harry's shoulders, and held her tight.

"Yes," said Mr. Jebb, very firm and quiet. "Think of her family, Ma. What if it were one of ours? Rich folk have feelings same as anyone else." But he looked very severely at Harry again. "*Did* you say you were beaten?" he asked her.

Harry nodded through her tears. They were tears of anger as much as anything. She had never in her life before been called such unkind things as Mrs. Jebb had just called her. "I get hit with a ruler when I get my sums wrong," she said. "I do. It

wasn't a lie. And I'm not selfish either. How was I
to know it would get you into trouble? *They*
should've known! If it's so terrible they jolly well
shouldn't have taken me!"

"Oh, Harry!" said Ned, taking his arm from around
her shoulder.

"You come with me, girl," said Mr. Jebb evenly.
And he took Harry by the hand, and led her off by
herself, down the towpath to a scruffy inn by the end

of the wharves. Outside the inn he called the potgirl who was gathering the dirty glasses from the tables in the yard, and taking her by the other hand, he walked the two of them a little way farther, and through a farm gate into the corner of a wheat field.

"Jessie," he said to the potgirl, "I've a particular reason for asking what I'm asking you today, and it's worth a sixpence to me, and perhaps a kinder heart to this young lady. But I'd like you to show her what you showed my Bess the last time we was past here." And then he turned his back and looked at the wheat. And the potgirl lifted her dress up over her head, and showed Harry a thin bony back with red weals on it, and smudgy black bruises.

"*That's* what it is to be beaten, my girl," said Mr. Jebb. And he gave Jessie a sixpence, and took Harry back to the boats without another word spoken.

After that it took the rest of the day for Mr. Jebb and three or four other men to shovel the coal from *Mary* and *Beatrice* out onto the paper mill wharf, and Harry was kept busy helping with the younger children, and peeling potatoes for supper. The next day was Sunday, with bells ringing from a church not far away, and the Jebbs put on Sunday clothes, carefully unfolded from stowage chests under the side beds in the cabins. Mr. Jebb wore corduroy trousers, almost white with much scrubbing, and a wide belt and suspenders embroidered all over in a pattern of spider webs in a dozen bright colors, and a shirt with a pattern of colored triangles and lozenges on it, just the same as the pattern on the cratches on his boats. Over his shirt he wore a mole-skin waistcoat with brass buttons and a velvet collar. Ned had clean shirt and trousers, and a spider-web belt, and a colored kerchief at his neck; Mrs. Jebb had a black satin dress, and a voluminous flower-sprigged bonnet, and a starched white apron;

and Bess had a ruched and frilled dress of brown and white check, and a clean white bonnet, and there was something crisp and clean for the three younger ones too, but Harry, whose clothes were dirty and torn, and who would not fit into anything of Bess's, had to be left behind in the boats. She sat alone and miserable, and polished some brassware in the cabin, hoping to please Mrs. Jebb.

Next day they turned the boats, in a specially widened part of the canal that Ned called a "winding hole," and started to take Harry home. The boats rode high out of the water, unladen as they were, and went along very smoothly and fast behind the horses, but even so with two animals and four boats to manage there was a lot to do, and Harry couldn't help with it, because Mrs. Jebb had taken all her clothes away, and she was wrapped in a blanket, sitting on a pile of roping and folded top cloths in the empty hold. Ned's small brother came and mocked her. "I hate you," he said. "We'll be hungry next week acause of you. And you look daft in that blanket."

But Ned said, "Don't worry, Harry, we've known worse. We was froze in for six weeks last winter, and down to our last hod of coal, and near starving afore the thaw. Bread and drippings in summer weather's nothing to that. *I* won't think hardly of you on account of that, honest!"

(73)

"Oh, Ned, I'm sorry, though, I'm terribly sorry!" said Harry. "If only there were something I could do."

As it turned out, there was something Harry could do. That evening after supper Mr. Jebb opened a drawer in the cabin of *Friendship* and brought out a Bible, very battered and tied together with ribbon. "I'm told you can read, young mistress," he said to Harry. "And it's seldom we get to hear from a book." So Harry opened his Bible very carefully and they all squeezed into the little cabin, and listened, and she read to them about Joseph and his brothers, and about David and Goliath, and about Noah's ark. Then Ned said to her, "I wish I could write me name, Harry."

"I'll show you," she said, eagerly.

"Would you show me mine, Harry?" said Bess.

"And mine, and mine," chorused the children.

Mrs. Jebb was sitting close by the lamp, mending something, but she raised her head and told Ned where he might find a stump of pencil, and Ned brought a bundle of toll tickets from the monkey drawer to serve as paper. Harry wrote the names large and clear, each on the back of a ticket, and set her pupils to copy them below, over and over. They passed the pencil around from hand to hand in silence. In a while Mr. Jebb pushed a blank ticket across the little flap-table to Harry, and said,

"Would you show me mine, girl?" Harry sat beside him, and guided his huge hand on its shaky course around WILLIAM JEBB over and over. And they worked at the writing till bedtime.

The next evening the pencil and tickets were brought out again, and again they set to work. "Do you want your name, Mrs. Jebb?" asked Harry, shyly.

"No, no, what use'd it be to me?" said Mrs. Jebb, shaking her head. But the next morning, while Harry was helping to dress the smallest child, Mrs. Jebb said, "What you could do, if you've a mind to it, is read my plates for me."

So Harry read the plates that hung all around the cabin of *Hope*. "A present from Brighton" said one. "God is not mocked" said another. There was a shiny sugar-pink plate with a picture of an iron bridge crossing from cliff to cliff over a river, which said "Clifton Suspension Bridge," and a jug with a picture of a little girl sitting on a trunk in a fur-edged cape, which said "Somebody's Luggage," and a china mug with pansies on it in relief, which said "Love the Giver." Mrs. Jebb became more and more pleased, and found Harry more things to read, right down to "Hankey and Sons" on the cast-iron stove, and "Made in Birmingham" on the brass coal scuttle.

On the last evening which Harry spent crammed into the little cabin with the Jebb family, Ned and Bess wrote so well that she showed them how to write *Mary* and *Beatrice* and *Hope* and *Friendship* as well as their names.

So the morning came when Harry woke to find the boats already moving, though it was dark still. As she wondered sleepily why, Ned came and shook her by the shoulder. "Wake up, Harry," he whispered, "wake up. This is where we took you up from, and you've got to go!"

When Harry scrambled out onto the deck, Mr. Jebb was waiting for her. He had his Bible laid on the open hatch. "You put your hand on that, and you swear to me, as you hope to live," he said to her, "that you'll not tell anyone—not anyone at all, not for any reason, my name, nor the name of my boats. You swear that, and you go safe home, and we go safe on our way."

Harry put her hand on the book and said, "I swear. Of course I won't tell," she added. "I wouldn't get you into trouble for anything after you've been so kind to me."

"You think what you'm doing and saying, another time, girl," said Mr. Jebb, smiling at her, "and fare you well now." And Ned said nothing, but pushed a folded toll ticket into her hand. Then he said, "Ger-rup, Rosie!" And the boats moved slowly away in the shadowy light of the very early morning, till they were out of sight among the dark willows on the canal-side.

And so Harry came home again, appearing in the

garden one morning before anyone but the kitchen-
maid was awake, suntanned and healthy, with
her clothes immaculately clean, and pressed, and the
tears in them mended in neat small stitches.

After the tremendous fuss had died down a bit,
Harry's family did try to make her say whom she had
been with. She would not. She told her father she
had been with the boat people, but had sworn an
oath not to name them. He told her very sternly what
terrible grief and worry she had caused; how they
had found her hat in the water, and dragged the cut

for her dead body, and found no trace of her. And
how her mother had been prostrate with shock and
sorrow all the time Harry had been gone. He hoped
she was very ashamed of herself. Harry was, she was.
And while she was apologizing with tears for the
grief she had caused at home, she let slip that she
had also caused hunger and hardship to the folk she
had been with, and then her father tried even harder
to make her say who they were, so that he could find
them, and offer them money to repay them for their
loss. But Harry felt quite sure that Mr. Jebb would

not be pleased by money that came from her broken word, so she still would not say, and her father could do nothing but thank God, and send a donation to an almshouse for retired boatmen run by the canal company.

.

"So there you are, Edward," said Harry, "that's what *I'm* like, and you might as well know it." She leaned over the picnic basket, and scooped the last of the potted shrimps onto her finger, and licked it slowly.

Edward grinned. "I assure you, dear Harry, that the manners of your rough companions have not in the least affected yours," he said.

"They weren't rough, Edward," said Harry sharply. "They were kind and gentle, and hard-working enough to deserve anyone's respect."

"Oh, *Harry*. Well, ignorant, then."

"Not that, either."

"You had to teach them to write their names, remember?"

"But look at what *I* didn't know; I didn't know where and how iron was made, or where the new railways went, or what sort of lives people lived making the things I used every day, as Ned knew; I hadn't seen the rivers open out to the sea, or the great ships loading from barges, or tunnels and factories, and all those things. Compared to him, I didn't know anything. But when I said that's what I'm like, I meant it—I mean I'm the sort who goes vagabond-ing. I mean to go to all sorts of far-off places and do all sorts of wild things in my life."

"Wherever you want to go, Harriet," said Edward, and he was looking at her very fondly, with a kind of shine in his eyes, "I'll take you."

"I don't want to be *taken,* Edward," said Harry softly. "I want to be *let go.*"

He looked away at once. Then he said, "Time to go home," and began to pick up the picnic things.

We were sleepy with sunlight and full of food, and we wandered slowly along the towpath, to the bridge that carried the lane up to the house.

"Harry," I asked her, "can you remember any of the songs Ned sang?"

"Well," she said, "there was one that went:

"Our commerce must thrive, and the arts soon revive,
Which are now in a sad situation,
If we follow this notion, from ocean to ocean,
To have a compleat navigation!

"And," she went on, "there was a very jolly one about 'The best of wrought metals is Birmingham ware!' and a very sad one about 'Oh, poor old horse!'"

Edward roared with laughter.

"And there was a nice one about 'Go where he will, he's my love still, my own dear navvy boy.'"

Harry was humming it softly, but Edward was still laughing and did not hear her.

"But wasn't it good to be home, Harry?" he said at last. "Wasn't it spacious and cozy and comfortable to be back again?"

"In a way. But I missed the cut too. It was still awfully dull at home most days, though they did send me on a day trip to the sea. They brought Susan back somehow—I don't know what her new employers must have thought—and as soon as they could, they moved a mile out of sight of the canal, where we are now. But until we went I used to sit in the garden watching the boats go by, and hoping and hoping to see *Mary* or *Beatrice* again. But I never did."

"I don't blame them for moving," said Edward.

"Well, they couldn't stop me lying in the grass in summer, thinking about it," said Harry, tossing her head. "Remembering the low light polishing the far end of the cut to green silver, and the trees hanging upside down on either side a reach of mirrored sky."

"Think of it in winter," said Edward.

We reached the bridge, and climbed up to the lane. Just beyond the bridge a pair of boats was tied up, waiting for the lock. A young woman stood at the tiller of one boat, and a handsome young man from another was sitting on the cabin roof, leaning toward her, and chatting. He was wearing a velvet-collared waistcoat like Mr. Jebb's Sunday best, and he had a

red kerchief around his neck, setting off his dark
curls. Harry looked keenly at him, pausing a moment
before she turned away. We left the canal behind us,
and trudged home.

.

That night while we ate our supper in Harry's old
schoolroom, I plucked up courage to ask her, "You're
not going to marry Edward, Harry, are you?"

"No, Kate," she said, "I'm not. How did you
know?"

"I just thought not," I said.

"Look, I'll show you something, Kate," she said. She went to her workbox, and felt in the silk lining, and brought out a little folded piece of dark green card. "TOLL at NAPTON TOP LOCK, one shilling a ton," it said.

And on the back, in shaky large round writing, *"Hope"* and *"Friendship"*